# POSEY Paints PRINCESS

by Harriet Ziefert ♥ art by Yukiko Kido

BLUE 🍎 APPLE

for Sylvie
- H.M.Z.

for Miyu and Mifu
- Y.K.

Text
copyright © 2008
by Harriet Ziefert

Illustrations
copyright © 2008
by Yukiko Kido

All rights reserved/CIP data is available.
Published in the United States 2013 by
🍎 Blue Apple Books, 515 Valley Street,
Maplewood, New Jersey 07040
www.blueapplebooks.com
Printed in China
07/13

ISBN: 978-1-60905-369-7
1 3 5 7 9 10 8 6 4 2

This is Posey. She likes pink.
And she likes to paint.

# Posey has lots of art supplies.

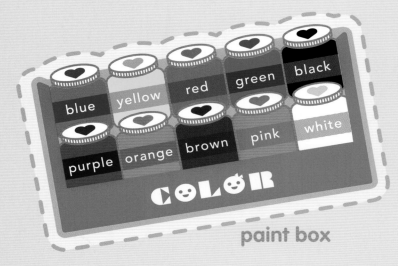

blue | yellow | red | green | black
purple | orange | brown | pink | white

COLOR

paint box

paintbrushes

water pots

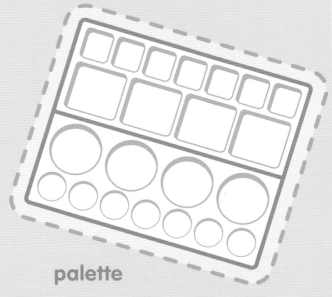

palette

Posey's friend Nina comes to visit.
She asks, "What should we do?"
Posey answers, "Let's paint."

Posey's mom
spreads newspaper
on the table.

Then she puts
a big piece of
white paper
in the middle.

Posey
and Nina
fill the
water pots.

Posey's mom gets five colors of paint— red, yellow, blue, black, and white.

Posey wants more colors. But her mom says, "Five are enough to make all the colors of the rainbow."

# Posey's mom shows them how to mix colors.

Do you know that a little **red** and a little **blue** makes **purple**?

A little red and a little **yellow** makes **orange**.

A little **blue** and a little **yellow** makes **green**.

**Black** makes a color darker; **white** makes a color lighter.

You have to add **black** slowly. If you add too much, it makes paint the color of mud!

"Look! A dab of red and a dot of **white**—mix them together and you have pink!" (That's Posey's favorite color.)

Sometimes
Posey puts
too much paint
on the brush.

She makes a
big blob and she gets
MAD!

Nina says, "Don't cry, Posey.
Everyone makes mistakes.
Sometimes you can fix a mistake."

Nina helps Posey turn the blob
into a strawberry ice cream sundae.

Then they start a new painting.
Posey paints on one side.

Nina paints
on the other.

Posey says, "I'm painting Princess.
Nina, what are you painting?"

"I'm painting a pickle," answers Nina.

"When she's hungry, Princess
can eat it," says Posey.

Then Posey says, "Every princess needs a crown! I'll make one."

"And every picture needs a sun!"
says Nina. "I'm painting one."

"You've been busy,"
says Posey's mom.
"What's the title
of your painting?"

Posey whispers to Nina, then she
answers, "The title is: Princess Pickle."

PRINCESS
PICKLE